THE MOOSEPIRE

Daniel Pinkwater

Little, Brown and Company
Boston   Toronto

First Edition

Library of Congress Cataloging-in-Publication Data
Pinkwater, Daniel Manus, 1941 —
    The moosepire.

    Summary: The talking blue moose attempts to unravel
the riddle of the Moosepire, a vampire moose that report-
edly lurks near the town of Yellow Tooth.
    [1. Moose — Fiction.   2. Vampires — Fiction.   I. Title.
PZ7.P6335Mo 1986   [Fic]   85–23843
ISBN 0–316–70811–9

AHS

*Published simultaneously in Canada
by Little, Brown & Company (Canada) Limited*

Printed in the United States of America

Books by Daniel Pinkwater

Ducks!

The Hoboken Chicken Emergency

Bear's Picture

Lizard Music

The Worms of Kukumlima

The Wuggie Norple Story

Tooth-Gnasher Superflash

Yobgorgle: Mystery Monster of Lake Ontario

Fat Men from Space

Alan Mendelsohn, the Boy from Mars

I Was a Second Grade Werewolf

The Snarkout Boys and the Avocado of Death

The Snarkout Boys and the Baconburg Horror

The Magic Moscow

Attila the Pun: A Magic Moscow Book

Slaves of Spiegel: A Magic Moscow Story

Young Adults

Blue Moose

Return of the Moose

The Moosepire

This is a story I was told by Sir Charles Pacamac, World's Champion Samovar Crasher. Sir Charles is a famous geographer. He had lectured at the University of London, where I met him when I was a very young man.

I was a guest of Sir Charles at his London club, the Amphibolus.

We were enjoying a cup of tea when the distinguished geographer said, "Pinkwater, you miserable half-wit, have I ever told you of my experience with the dreaded Vampire Moose of North America?"

"No, Sir Charles," I said. "In fact, I've never heard of such a thing as a Vampire Moose. What is it?"

"I tell you, Pinky, it is a dreadful creature," Sir Charles said. "Not many men have ever seen one — and even fewer have lived to tell the tale. I encountered one in the wilds of North America a number of years ago. It was a remarkable experience — but even more remarkable was another moose I met at about the same time. This moose spoke very good English and he was as blue as . . . as . . . as an onion — ever hear of anything like that, Pinkwater, you ragamuffin?"

In fact, I had not only heard of the famous Blue Moose, but had written two books about him. However, I could not expect a distinguished person such as Sir Charles Pacamac to have any interest in my unimportant writings, so I politely asked, "Blue as an onion?"

"Well, blue as a what-do-you-call-it then. Confound it man, the moose was blue! Blue as an asparagus! And he spoke like a gentleman — which is more than I can say for you, Pinkwater, you drooling idiot. Do you want to hear this story or not?"

"Certainly, Sir Charles," I said, sipping my cup of Lapsang Souchong and puffing my cheroot.

"Then stop that blasted sipping and puffing. You make me nervous!" said the wonderful old Englishman.

"I'd like to hear the story very much," I said.

"Very well — if you insist," said Sir Charles. "Make yourself comfortable. I'll summon the serving wallah. Yitzhak! Bring Pinkwater Bwana a baked potato! You may as well have a snack — this story will take some time."

The Pakistani waiter brought me a baked potato on a stick, and I settled back in my leather armchair, and listened to Sir Charles's remarkable account:

"I was studying a plague of gerbils in the Northern Territory. In order to be near the subject of my study, I had to put up in a primitive little town called Yellowtooth in the back of beyond. It was forty degrees below freezing in the shade, and the most congenial entertainment available to the locals was sucking on chunks of ice and then trying to whistle.

"I had taken a room at the local hotel, a vile place called the Morpheus Arms. In the evening, I would descend to the taproom for a

saucer of fermented mare's milk. There I engaged the natives in conversation. It appeared they were all afraid of some ghostly animal — a moose of tremendous size, with glowing eyes and fangs. All of them swore they had seen it — or knew someone who had. It sounded like a load of tapioca to me.

"The inhabitants of Yellowtooth called this imaginary moose Deadly Eric — or Eric the Dead. They believed he was a sort of moose zombie, a walking deadster. Eric was supposed to lie in wait for solitary travelers and then leap upon them and suck the wax out of their ears, causing them to go insane or worse. This is the sort of balderdash people always tell in remote places where there is nothing to do. I was mildly amused and did nothing to discourage this harmless belief of the simple inhabitants of Yellowtooth.

"Then, one night, I was just about to go to bed when I saw something amazing through the window. Standing in the middle of the main street of Yellowtooth, bathed in moonlight — bright as an onion — was the largest moose I had even seen. When I say that this moose was large, I want you to understand that all moose are large. Large might almost be a synonym for moose. This moose was gigantic! He was as big as an . . . as an . . . as an onion! This moose was as big as a big, colossal, enormous, gigantic, oversized, vast, impossible, huge onion — if you can imagine that. Well? Don't just sit there sucking on that baked potato, man! Do you understand what I'm talking about or not, you blasted nudnik?"

"The moose was as large as an onion," I said. "If an onion were to be of stupendous size."

"Yes. That's it exactly," said Sir Charles. "Now let me get on with my story. No more interruptions, please. As I said, there was this really big moose, just standing in the middle of the street. He had eyes that glowed like onions, and he had sharp fangs. I can tell you, I would rather have faced a rhino in my shorts than deal with that fellow.

"However, I pride myself on remaining cool in a crisis. I had my camera at hand — I'd been photographing the gerbils, you see — and I screwed in a flashbulb and let fly. I got three or

four pictures of the brute before he turned and sauntered out of town, just as fearless as an . . . as an . . . as an . . .”

"As an onion?" I put in.

"As an onion? That doesn't make sense at all. Are you sure you're following this story?"

I said I was.

"Then kindly don't keep breaking in with irrelevancies. Now, where was I? Oh, yes, the moose was fearless as an eggplant, and he just walked out of town. I was down to the chemist's like a shot the next morning to have my photos developed.

"The photos were remarkable. I had extra wallet-size prints made and sent them on the next dogsled to my friend, Professor Anton Wildebeeste at the University of Saskatoon. The professor arrived in person five days later. He was very excited. 'If this is what it appears to be,' said Professor Wildebeeste, 'that is, if these photographs are really of Eric the Dead — then they prove something very important.'

" 'What is that?' I asked.

" 'They prove that he really exists! For years

I too have heard the legends, but had hoped they were not true. You see, there was no evidence — no proof. Now, with these photographs, we have to assume that this monster moose is real. Do you think he is dangerous?'

" 'He looked dangerous. I had the feeling that he was dangerous. I would say, yes. Yes, he is dangerous.'

" 'I think he is dangerous too,' said Professor Wildebeeste.

" 'The local people all think he is dangerous,' I said.

" 'You didn't show them the photographs?' Professor Wildebeeste asked.

" 'No, I didn't want to frighten them,' I said.

" 'Good. That is good. They can do nothing. There is no reason to cause panic. Also, we can do nothing. There is only one person who can save civilization from this terrible Deadly Eric — and that person . . . is not . . . a . . . person.'

" 'Not a person?' I asked. 'Then what?'

" 'The only being known to me who can

deal with this horrible monster moose,' said Professor Wildebeeste, 'is a moose himself.'

"I was amazed. I did not believe my ears. Surely, my old friend Professor Wildebeeste could not mean what he said.

" 'Surely you do not mean it,' I said. 'You believe that a moose is the only person to deal with this monster?'

" 'That's what I said, Sir Charles,' the professor said. 'I would like you to meet this remarkable moose. Will you come with me?'

"So the professor took me to meet this Blue Moose, and we had a chat with him. I must say that even though he was a quadruped, he had very good manners, almost as though he were an Englishman himself. Still, I had misgivings about trusting a beast with fur and antlers, but the professor assured me that the moose was all right.

" 'I will look into this matter,' the Blue Moose said.

" 'But what are you going to do?' I asked.

" 'Professor Wildebeeste knows my methods,' the moose said. 'He will explain to you that I prefer to work alone and in secret.'

" 'But can you do anything about the Vampire Moose?' I asked.

" 'That remains to be seen. First I must do some research.'

" 'But no one has ever seen Eric the Dead before!' Professor Wildebeeste shouted. 'Where can you do research about an imaginary monster?'

" 'I'll start in the usual place,' the moose said.

" 'And where is that?'

" 'The public library, of course,' the moose said.

"I suppose the moose went to the library. I'm dashed if I know what he found out there. I never saw him or the monster again. A year or two later, Professor Wildebeeste wrote to me to say that the Blue Moose had taken care of the Deadly Eric business. Amazing, what?"

"But how did the Blue Moose deal with the monster — the Vampire Moose?" I asked Sir Charles.

"No idea, old fig — just a deuced amazing critter, that moose. Spoke as well as an English-man — better than you, Pinky. Amazing story, what?"

"You mean you never found out exactly what happened?" I asked.

"No. I finished my work on the wild ger-bils, and packed up and came back to London. I just thought you'd like to hear about the Blue Moose — unusual animal."

I knew then what I had to do. I had to find out what had happened when the Blue Moose met Deadly Eric. I would go to Yellowtooth at once and begin tracking down the story. I made preparations to leave.

"I have to leave now, Sir Charles," I said.

"Fine, fine, young man," Sir Charles said. "Just have that hundredweight of onions deliv-ered to my town address."

"Onions?" I asked.

"Yes. Aren't you the man from the whole-sale greengrocers?"

"No, Sir Charles," I said. "I am Daniel

Pinkwater, famous author and noted moose-ologist."

"I never heard such rot in my life," said Sir Charles. "Just pay for your baked potato and get out of my sight."

I set fire to Sir Charles's walking stick, and left the adorable old Englishman musing over his memories in the Amphibolus Club. Later that day I left London. I took a plane. Then I took a train. . . . Then I took a bus. Then I took a dogsled. . . . Then I walked on snowshoes. In three days I was in Yellowtooth. I remembered what the Blue Moose had said about the best place to begin one's research. I went straight to the public library.

I was afraid the library might be closed, because all of the citizens appeared to be at the ice-sucking and whistling finals in the school gymnasium. However, I was in luck. The library was open and the head librarian was there. Mildred Beeswax was the head librarian, a handsome woman of eighty or ninety years of age.

"I am Daniel Pinkwater, famous author and noted mooseologist," I said.

"I know all about that," Mildred Beeswax said. "You wrote those silly books about the Blue Moose."

"Ah," I said, flattered, "then you have my books in this library?"

"No."

"Not even one?"

"No. I won't have them in my library. We have standards here."

"I see. Of course. Um. Well, in fact it is about the Blue Moose that I have come to see you."

"I don't know why that moose doesn't sue you for defamation of character," Mildred Beeswax said. "If you ever put me in a book, sonny, you'd better put down everything I say, and make sure you get it right."

"Certainly," I said to the librarian. "So you remember the Blue Moose?"

"Of course I do, pipsqueak," Mildred Beeswax said. "What do you want to know about him?"

"I believe he came here once to do some research."

"Yes. He came here when he was called in on the case of Deadly Eric, the Vampire Moose," Mildred Beeswax said.

"That's what I want to know about," I said. "What happened then?"

"I have no idea, tubby," the librarian said. "I was out that week with the Book-mo-sled, delivering literature to the goldminers up in the hills. What a bunch of rascals! Wheee!"

"You weren't here?"

"No, goofus — my assistant, Matilda Flintwhistle, was in charge when the Blue Moose turned up. I'm sorry I missed him. On the other hand, I had a lot of fun up at the diggings."

"And where is Ms. Flintwhistle?" I asked.

"She wandered off during the thaw one year," Mildred Beeswax said. "Poor dear. I don't know what became of her."

"So I've come all the way from London, traveling by plane, train, dogsled, and snow-shoes, having eaten nothing but a baked potato in the past three days, and the only person who might remember the Blue Moose's visit is gone, and you don't know *where*?"

"That's right, dope," Mildred Beeswax said. "You'd have saved some trouble if you'd telephoned from London. We answer questions by telephone, you know."

"So there's no way for me to find out what happened when the Blue Moose came here!"

"Not unless you read the manuscript he sent us."

"The moose sent you a manuscript?"

"Yes. It's sort of a diary of the case of Deadly Eric."

"And you've got it here?"

"Certainly."

"And I can see it?"

"Are your hands clean?"

"I washed them on the dogsled."

"Then yes, you may."

Mildred Beeswax led me to a table and brought me a blue notebook. It was written in longhoof. This is what I read:

The Case of the Vampire Moose

In order to escape unwanted publicity created by the books written by that fool, Pinkwater, I was forced to move to the northernmost wilderness. Fortunately, not many copies of the books were sold, and it looked as though I would be able to return to my normal life in a short time.

I was terribly bored in the Northland. There wasn't much to do beyond sucking chunks of ice and trying to whistle. I was grateful when I received a visit from my old friend, Professor Anton Wildebeeste of the University of Saskatoon. He had with him an English naturalist, Sir Charles Pacamac, whom I remembered as the World's Champion Samovar Crasher. I was honored to meet the great athlete.

It developed that Professor Wildebeeste wanted my help in the matter of a vampire moose that had been terrorizing a small community — Yellowtooth. I promised Professor Wildebeeste that I would deal with the matter, and left for Yellowtooth at once.

Arriving in the miserable little town, I realized that I had no idea how to deal with this matter. I had never seen or heard of a vampire moose that sucked ear wax and terrorized people. In fact, with few exceptions, moose are superior animals, good members of society, and lots of fun. I spent some time in conversation with the locals, but found them to be a superstitious lot with very little solid information to share about the vampire other than his name — Deadly Eric.

I turned to my usual starting point in any research — the public library — where I found Matilda Flintwhistle, the helpful assistant librarian. Ms. Flintwhistle told me I had free run of the library. I went right to work.

My first stop was the good old card catalog. I looked up books on vampires, the history of vampires, vampire hunting, vampires in art, literature, movies, and television, and vampires named Eric. Also, in the crafts section, books on how to make a vampire out of clay, wood, and papier-mâché. I also looked up books on large land animals of North America, the natural history of the deer family (to which moose belong), famous moose in history, a book called *Who's Moose,* a novel called *Forever Antler,* and, of course, the *Moose Scout Handbook.* I was pleased to see how many books there were about moose. I wrote down the title, author, and number of each book on a separate little piece of paper.

Some books I needed were not in the public library of Yellowtooth — for example those awful books by that idiot, Pinkwater. To be thorough, I thought I'd better read them, so I asked Ms. Flintwhistle to order them for me on interlibrary loan.

I also asked Ms. Flintwhistle to look up the number of citizens of Yellowtooth who had gone mad in the past ten years — with special emphasis on those who had gone mad after an encounter with a supernormal moose. I also looked up books on madness, earwax, psychoneurosis, the treatment of insane people, people who have had strange experiences, and folktales about big animals who jump out of the dark at people and do nasty things to them.

Then I looked up books of geography, the history of the area around Yellowtooth, and the

diaries of early settlers in the vicinity. I planned to look through these diaries for any mention of the Vampire Moose.

I also looked up books about the legends of the local Indian people for the same purpose.

In order to be prepared to deal with the Vampire Moose when I met him, I looked up books on trapping, hunting, building traps, self-defense, how to overpower huge angry animals, and first aid.

As I found the card for each book, I wrote down the number, author, and title. By this time I had filled a considerable number of little pieces of paper.

Then, in the encyclopedias and dictionaries, I looked up moose, vampires, legends, madness, trapping, fighting, moose with the name Eric, and methods for dealing with supernatural beings. I also looked at microfilms of old newspaper articles. While I was doing this, Ms. Flintwhistle was finding the books I had noted on my pieces of paper. There were 962 of them.

However, I was not yet finished. In the phonograph record department, I listened to a record

of moose calls, and an opera called *Fledermoose.*
I also listened in to Ms. Flintwhistle reading a
story to some children who had come to the
library. The story was about a moose named
Heinrich. It was nice to be read to. I sat on the
floor with the children and had a pleasant time.

I then checked out the 962 books. (Ms.
Flintwhistle had issued me a temporary library
card.)

By this time evening was approaching, and
there was to be a film shown at the library. I
stayed and watched it. It was called *Mushroom
Gathering in the Andes.* I had never seen it before. Amazingly, it turned out to be my lifetime
favorite movie. It showed the happy people of
the high mountains, going around looking for
mushrooms! It was wonderful! The narration
told all about mushrooms and how to find them.
I made a note to come back to the library after
I had dealt with the vampire moose, and check
out some books about mushrooms, amateur
mushroom growing, mushroom culture for profit,
South America, the Andes Mountains, films, film-
making, fungi, poisonous fungi, how to recog-

nize poisonous fungi, and what to do if you accidently eat a poisonous fungus.

I then took the 962 books to the empty boxcar on the deserted railway siding where I was staying. I could have taken a room at the Morpheus Arms, but I wanted to come and go unseen. Also, the boxcar didn't cost anything, and rooms at the Morpheus Arms cost $1.75 a day.

The first thing I did after I had settled into my boxcar with my 962 library books was to write a letter to my friend, Mr. Breton.

Mr. Breton is my employer. I help him run his restaurant. I also get to live in a room upstairs for free. I like Mr. Breton, and the restaurant, and my room. I would never have left home but for the unwanted publicity brought by the books written by that infernal Daniel Pinkwater.

The truth is, I was feeling a little homesick. This is the letter I wrote my friend and employer, Mr. Breton:

Dear Chef,
I am solving the case of a vampire

moose here in the frozen North. I have begun my research on the subject.

I will write to you from time to time.

There may be danger, but it is my duty to do all I can to help man and moosekind.

Please say hello to Dave, the hermit, and Mr. Bobowicz, the game warden.

I wish I had a bowl of your clam chowder.

Your friend,

The Moose

The Moose

I felt a bit better after writing the letter. Then I settled down to read the books I had checked out. I had a few dozen onions for supper. There was a bright full moon, so I was able to read far into the night.

By the next morning, I had read 943 of the library books. I now knew nearly everything about

vampires, vampire hunting, vampires in art, literature, movies, and television, vampires named
Eric, how to make a vampire out of clay, wood,
and papier-mâché, large land animals of North
America, the natural history of the deer family,
famous moose in history, how to tie moose knots,
various statistics regarding madness and moose
in Yellowtooth, insanity, spooky animals, local
history, trapping, hunting, self-defense, and how
to overpower huge angry animals.

My next step was to set about capturing
Eric the Dead himself. To this end, I searched
the woods for signs of the Vampire Moose. I
knew what to look for because I'd read the books.
There was not a single sign of a vampire moose —
or a vampire — or a moose (other than myself).

I took to lurking around the town of Yellowtooth, listening under windows and in public
places for some mention of Deadly Eric. Nothing
special. Nobody had seen the monster lately, and
the conversation about him was getting stale.

There was nothing to do but wander the
woods, waiting and thinking. I did so. I wandered. I thought. I studied the features of the

forest — the moss, the grasses, the trees, the little woodland creatures. This was somewhat boring for me. As a moose, I already knew all about that sort of thing. But there was still no sign of the Vampire Moose, so I had nothing to do but wait.

I must admit I was getting lonely, and I was grateful when Nathan of the North showed up. Nathan of the North was an old prospector, mountain man, trapper, scout, mule driver, hunter, and conservative Jewish Rabbi. He knew a lot about life in the woods, and also Talmudic commentary. Nathan taught me the blessing for onions-and-moss soup.

Nathan asked whether he could stay with me in my boxcar. I told him I would be only too glad to have some company. He moved in with his traps and prayer books, and a chicken he'd picked up somewhere along the trail.

I asked Nathan of the North if he knew anything about the Vampire Moose.

"I'll look it up," he said.

Nathan of the North reported to me that there was nothing in any of his books of Hebrew lore and philosophy, except for a brief reference to a bagel vampire called Noshferatu.

"You know, there was nothing specific about Deadly Eric or any vampire moose in any of the stuff I took out of the library either," I said.

"Are you sure the Moosepire isn't fictional?" Nathan of the North asked me. "For it is written (somewhere), a thing isn't a thing unless it is a thing."

"Did you bring any of those Jewish crackers?" I asked Nathan.

"Matzohs, also known as matzoth?" Nathan replied. "I have some in my pack. We shall sit here in the wilderness and eat matzohs or matzoth, for it is written (but I forget where) that we shall sit in the wilderness and eat matzohs. Or matzoth."

Nathan of the North was a nice chap, and I was glad for his company — but I could see he was going to be no help at all in catching the Vampire Moose.

"Maybe you should use some sort of bait to catch him," Nathan said. "What does he like?"

"I hear he likes ear wax," I said.

"Yicch!" said Nathan of the North.

"Well, I'm going to go and look around for him one more time," I said.

"Fine," said Nathan. "I'll stay here and say my prayers and then make some birch-bark tea and fungus and lichen stew."

"Yicch!" I said.

I had looked everywhere possible for Deadly Eric, not once but ten times. I was pretty discouraged. I decided that my best bet was to lurk in town and try to overhear things. I also liked lurking better because a town, even Yellowtooth, is more interesting to me than the great wilderness.

It may be hard to believe but a moose, large as it is, can be a very successful lurker — and I, a trained detective, can make myself almost invisible when there is need. Thus I was able to go in and out of town on many lurking forays without being seen by the local inhabitants.

I would skulk into Yellowtooth, keeping within the shadows, and making no noise. Then I would listen at keyholes and under windows trying to catch some word that would help me find Deadly Eric. I also peeked into windows whenever possible, in hope of catching a glimpse of the Vampire Moose. When there was danger of being discovered, I would freeze — become utterly motionless, and blend into the darkness.

On rare occasions, I would abandon my concealment, and speak to a responsible-looking citizen. Actually, I only did this once. A fellow was emerging from a place of entertainment, and I casually walked alongside and whispered directly in his ear, "Sir, have you any information regarding the Vampire Moose, Eric the Dead? It would be a great help to me if — "

At this point, the silly fellow gave a scream and ran off into the night, shouting nonsense about Eric. An idiot of some sort, it appeared. I abandoned my idea of getting information directly from the natives.

One night, shortly after Nathan of the North had come to stay with me, someone photographed me on one of my nightly lurks. There was a flash — then another. Someone was taking my picture with the aid of a flashbulb. I stood still. I had nothing to fear, after all — I was doing

no wrong. To run away would have been to draw attention to myself. I hoped the pictures had been taken by an enterprising tourist wanting a souvenir of the Northland. In my mind I congratulated the photographer on having found a moose-subject as handsome as myself. They would be prize-winning pictures, I thought.

When I arrived back at the boxcar, I found my friend Nathan admiring some black-and-white photographs. What a coincidence.

"These are fine pictures of you, my friend," Nathan of the North said.

"Let me see," I said. "Yes, they are rather good." For a moment I thought that somehow Nathan had gotten hold of the pictures the unknown tourist had taken that very night — but how could that have been possible? "Wait!" I said. "These are not pictures of me. These are the pictures of Deadly Eric, the Moosepire, taken by Sir Charles Pacamac, and given to me by my friend Professor Anton Wildebeeste."

"No, no!" said Nathan of the North. "My practiced trapper's and rabbi's eye is not to be deceived. These are pictures of you, Moose — I have no doubt."

I examined the pictures. "You know, they do look like me," I admitted.

"It is you," Nathan said. "It looks exactly like you. Besides, what other moose wears eyeglasses?"

"But these are pictures of the Vampire Moose!" I said. "I am confused."

"Unless . . ." said Nathan of the North.

"Unless?" I asked, wondering.

"Unless, *you* are the Vampire Moose," Nathan of the North said.

"But how could that be?" I asked.

"Now I am confused," said Nathan of the North.

We pondered the question. We pondered for three days and three nights. At the end of that time, we still had not come up with an acceptable theory that would explain how I could be the moose in the photographs of Deadly Eric, the Vampire Moose, which Sir Charles Pacamac had taken.

We stopped pondering for a snack. Nathan of the North prepared a huge quantity of pinecone soup and Jewish crackers. I had fifteen bowls,

and Nathan of the North had eleven. We ate so much that we could barely move.

Then Nathan of the North took to pacing. First he walked up and down, trying to figure out the mystery of how I could be in the photos of the Vampire Moose. Then he paced in circles. Then he paced around and around the boxcar. Then he paced through the boxcar, entering it by the door on the north end, and coming out the door on the south end.

"Aren't you getting hungry?" Nathan of the North asked. "I could eat a whole lot of pinecone soup and matzos or matzoth right now."

"You just had eleven bowls of the stuff," I said. "How could you be hungry already?"

"Nonsense," said Nathan of the North. "I haven't eaten much of anything for the past three days while we've been trying to figure out this mystery."

"You don't remember eating?"

"I didn't eat. I'm starving. I'm empty."

"Impossible," I said.

"But true," said Nathan of the North.

"I have a sort of dim idea," I said. "Sit right there, and don't move."

I scribbled a note and tied it to my right hoof. Then I galloped through the north door of the boxcar, and came out the south door. "I'm hungry," I said.

Then I noticed the note. "What's this?" I said. I read the note:

If you don't remember having written this note, go into the door on the south side of the boxcar, and come out the door on the north side — but first, write on the bottom of the note whether you are hungry or not. This is serious. Do it!

I wrote "hungry" at the bottom of the note, and galloped into the door on the south side of the boxcar and out the door on the north side. When I came out, I remembered why I had written the note in the first place — and the word I had added at the bottom proved my theory. I burped.

"Nathan of the North, I have solved the mystery!" I said.

"I'm hungry," said Nathan of the North.

My experiment had worked. My theory was proven. The boxcar was actually some sort of time machine — and if one entered it by the north side and emerged from the south side, one would go back in time. If one entered the boxcar from the south door and came out the north door, one would go forward in time.

I remembered remarking to myself when I first found the boxcar that I had never seen any railroad equipment made out of what I took to be shiny aluminum that glowed green at night. "This boxcar is a thing from another time, or planet even," I said to Nathan of the North.

"You know, I'm going to die if I don't eat something soon," Nathan said. "How long do I have to sit here?"

"I beg your pardon," I said. "Just pass through that door, keep going, and come out the other side."

"Why?"

"Because I ask you to — and it is written in some book of wisdom or other, 'He who does not oblige his friend will get no soup.' "

Nathan did as I asked. He entered the boxcar by the door on the north side and came out of the one on the south side.

"Ready for a big meal?" I asked him.

"Are you crazy?" Nathan of the North asked me. "I'm so full of soup I'm afraid I might plotz, or explode."

"This is most remarkable," I said.

"What is?" asked Nathan of the North.

"I have figured out how it can be that I am the Vampire Moose."

"You have?"

"Yes."

"So?"

"So what?"

"So how is it possible?"

"This is how. The boxcar is a time machine."

"It is?"

"It is. You go in one door and come out the other, and you will go back and forth in time. I haven't quite figured out how to operate the thing — but we just had a demonstration."

"We did?"

"We did. You ate a lot, walked in one door and out the other, and all of a sudden you were hungry again — why?"

"Why? Tell me."

"I'll tell you. You went back in time to just before you ate."

"So I was hungry again."

"Exactly. Later, when you went through the time machine in the other direction, you went forward in time to the present — after having eaten — so you weren't hungry."

"So I wasn't hungry." Nathan of the North was trying to take it all in. "But how does this make you Deadly Eric?"

"Somehow, I went a good deal further back in time, and turned up in Yellowtooth. Sir Charles Pacamac took some photos of me with a flash-bulb. He thought I was Deadly Eric.

"When I whispered in a citizen's ear, he took it to be the Vampire Moose trying to suck the wax out of his ears, and this added to the general panic."

"So who is the real Moosepire?" Nathan of the North asked.

"You mean other than me? There is no Moosepire other than me."

"How can you be sure?" Nathan of the North asked.

"Well I can't be one hundred percent sure," I said. "But none of my research at the public library turned up any evidence of there being a real Moosepire. The only photos of the Moosepire look just like me. We seem to have stumbled on a time machine, and . . ."

"Where do you suppose that came from?" asked Nathan of the North.

"I was wondering that myself," I said. "It may have been left here by some time traveler — or it might have gotten away from whoever owns it."

"You were saying about the Moosepire."

"You know, Nathan of the North, I am bored with the Moosepire, aren't you?"

"Well, now that we both believe it was you all the time, it is quite boring — but to tell the truth, I was bored from the beginning."

"I will send a postcard to Professor Wildebeeste, and tell him the Vampire Moose business is settled. There is no need to go into the details — it might be embarrassing. Then let's see if we can learn to work this time machine."

"Do you suppose we can get it to take us

to the eighteenth century?" Nathan of the North asked. "I've always wanted to go there."

"We can see," I said. "Theoretically, it should be able to take us to any time period at all. Do you have any desire to see the distant future?"

"Can we see the eighteenth century too?"

"Why not?"

"Well, if we can go to both, I have no objection to visiting the distant future."

Nathan of the North and I began our study of the time machine. We soon had a fairly good idea of how it worked, and we prepared to become time travelers. Our first experiment was . . .

Here the manuscript abruptly ended. I asked the librarian, Mildred Beeswax, if there had been any more pages.

"That's all there is, bozo," the librarian said. "Now haul your fat little self out of here — it's closing time."

I left the library and went out into the streets of Yellowtooth. I had traveled through vast wilderness, I had been subjected to insults, and I had starved, and suffered from reader's cramp —

but I had found out the true story of the Moose-pire. What was more, I was now ready to write another book about the Blue Moose, and earn fame and vast sums of money by doing so.

Sucking on an icicle I had broken off the library building, I made my way to the highway, to hitch a ride on a passing dogsled.